THE THREE LITTLE FISH

FOR MARTHA—K.G.

FOR MY FISHY IVY,
WHO MAKES HER HOUSE OUT OF FABRIC,
FOR MY FISHY RALEIGH,
WHO MAKES HIS HOUSE OUT OF SKATEBOARDS
AND FOR MY FISHY RUSSELL,
WHO MAKES HIS HOUSE OUT OF MAGIC!

—J.G.

BIG BAD SHARK

ISBN-13: 978-0-439-71963-6
ISBN-10: 0-439-71963-1

11 10 9 8 7 6 5 4 3 2 1   09 10 11 12 13

Printed in the U.S.A.
This edition first printing, January 2009

BY **KEN GEIST**

ILLUSTRATED BY **JULIA GORTON**

Cartwheel B·O·O·K·S ®

SCHOLASTIC INC.

NEW YORK   TORONTO   LONDON   AUCKLAND   SYDNEY
MEXICO CITY   NEW DELHI   HONG KONG   BUENOS AIRES

ONCE UPON A TIME, THERE LIVED A MAMA FISH AND HER THREE LITTLE FISH, JIM, TIM, AND KIM. "IT IS NOW TIME," SAID THE MAMA, "FOR EACH OF YOU TO MAKE A HOME IN THE DEEP BLUE SEA." SO OFF THEY WENT.

"TAKE AS MUCH AS YOU CAN CARRY," SAID THE SEA HORSE.

JIM GATHERED THE SEAWEED AND MADE A WEEDY LITTLE HOUSE.

JIM HAD JUST FINISHED BUILDING HIS SEAWEED HOUSE WHEN HE HEARD THE BIG BAD SHARK KNOCKING AT THE DOOR.

"LITTLE FISH, LITTLE FISH, LET ME COME IN."

SO THE BIG BAD SHARK MUNCHED AND HE CRUNCHED AND HE ATE UP EVERY BIT OF THE SEAWEED HOUSE.

AND JIM SWAM AWAY—JUST IN TIME.

TO WHICH THE BRAVE LITTLE FISH REPLIED,

"NOT BY THE SKIN OF MY FINNY FIN FIN!"

"THEN I'LL MUNCH AND I'LL CRUNCH AND I'LL SMASH YOUR HOUSE IN," ROARED THE SHARK.

So the BIG BAD SHARK MUNCHED AND HE CRUNCHED UNTIL HE GOT A SANDY MOUTHFUL AND THE HOUSE CRUMBLED.

"THE **BIG BAD SHARK** DESTROYED **OUR** HOUSES."

"**DON'T** WORRY. YOU **CAN** LIVE WITH ME," SAID KIM. AND **THEY** DID.

THE THREE LITTLE FISH HAD JUST FINISHED LUNCH WHEN THEY HEARD THE BIG BAD SHARK KNOCKING AT THEIR DOOR.

"LITTLE FISH, LITTLE FISH, LET ME COME IN."

TO WHICH THE SMART FISH REPLIED,

"NOT BY THE SKIN OF MY FINNY FIN FIN!"

"THEN I'LL MUNCH AND I'LL CRUNCH AND I'LL SMASH YOUR HOUSE IN," ROARED THE SHARK.

THE BIG BAD SHARK
MUNCHED AND HE
CRUNCHED
BUT HE COULD NOT
SMASH THE HOUSE IN...

AND
ALL HIS TEETH
FELL OUT!

THE THREE LITTLE FISH WERE SAFE AT LAST.

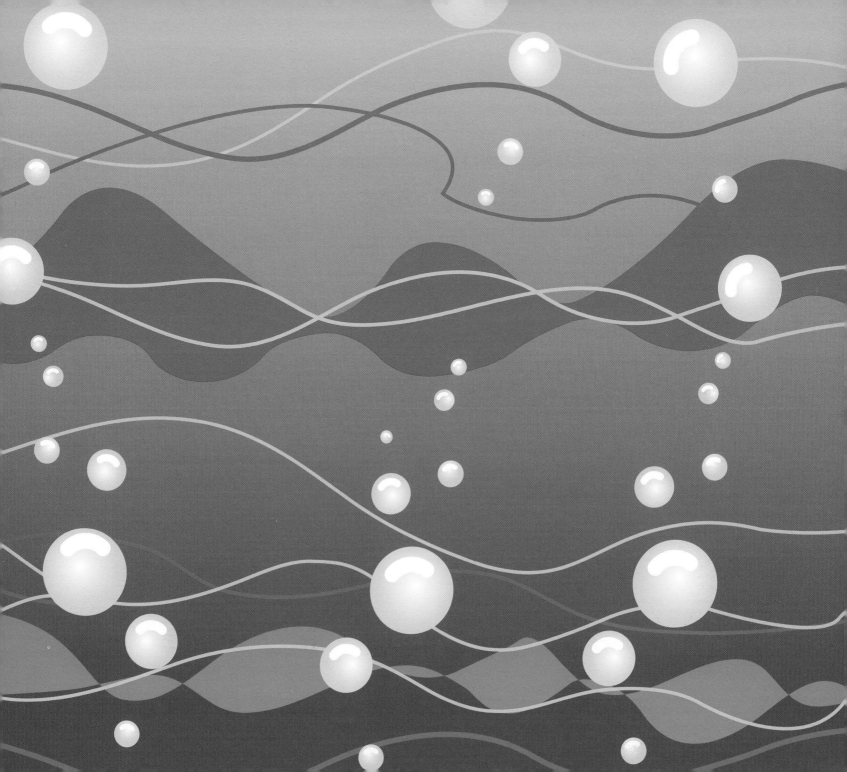